Tom & Jerry™

FAT-FREE CAT

Written by Stephen Thraves
Illustrated by Mick Hall

CARNIVAL

Tom chased Jerry round the living room, even more anxious to catch him than he usually was. The housekeeper had warned Tom that if he hadn't disposed of that mouse by the end of the week, she would be replacing him with a new cat. So Tom chased Jerry as fast as his legs would carry him, with a look of desperation on his face. He could be out on the street! But that pesky mouse was just too fast for him.

The thought of having to leave his nice cosy basket by the fire spurred Tom a bit. As did the thought of having to live in a cold dirty alley with all the mangy dogs picking on him. But the fact remained that either that little pest was getting faster, or Tom was getting slower.

With a good few metres to spare, Jerry nipped into the safety of his hole! "It must be *me* that's getting slower," Tom panted as he studied himself in a mirror. "Just look how fat I've become. I'm going to have to go on a diet."

Now this was something Tom had never done before and he was horrified by the idea. Going on a diet meant eating less cakes and whipped cream. Less jelly and fried fish. But if he didn't do something drastic, the only fish he would eating would be smelly heads and bones from the dustbin!

Fortunately, the housekeeper was a little on the plump side herself, so there were plenty of slimming books lying around the house. Tom picked one of them up, flicking through the pages. His face fell as he did so. He had to give up all his favourite foods. Instead of a saucer of cream, he had to drink fat-free milk. Instead of a slice of chocolate cake, he had to eat boring bread.

After a whole afternoon of this miserable diet, Tom could hear his stomach begin to gurgle. *POY-OY-OY-ONG* it rumbled. *PIY-IY-IY-ING*. What he would give for a double scoop ice-cream sundae... but no! He was determined - he had to catch that mouse!

And soon came his chance, for Jerry suddenly appeared out of his mousehole. Tom artfully watched him tip-toe across the room, waiting his moment. The diet had certainly made him hungrier, but had it also made him fitter? He patted his empty stomach. He was sure it had!

"YEE-AARGHH!" Tom roared as he suddenly sprang from his basket, bounding after his unsuspecting victim. Jerry nearly jumped out of his skin and immediately hared back towards his hole. He had a good start on Tom but the delighted cat could feel himself getting closer and closer by the second. He eagerly stretched out his paws, ready to pluck Jerry off his frantic little feet. But Jerry just reached his hole in time!

Tom wasn't too upset. "The diet's working!" he told himself with a grin, as he listened to Jerry panting inside the hole. "Just a bit more of it and I'll be able to overtake that little pest. He won't escape me next time!"

"Oh, won't I?" Jerry thought, when he had at last recovered his breath. He wiped the trickle of sweat from his brow. "We'll see about that!"

Waiting until Tom was back in his basket and there were loud snores coming from that direction, Jerry tip-toed into the kitchen. He scampered towards the refrigerator and tugged open the door. There was a huge wedge of his favourite cheese in there but he completely ignored it.

He wasn't interested in stuffing himself - just that persistent cat!

"Now, we'll see if he can resist *this!*" sniggered Jerry as he dragged a huge trifle from the fridge and pushed it towards Tom's basket, leaving it right under his nose. Then he tipped Tom's saucer of fat-free milk into a nearby plant pot. "And he'll *love* this!" he tittered as he replaced it with thick double cream.

He spooned some of the trifle into Tom's open mouth, just to get him going.

To begin with, Tom's sleepy tongue happily licked round his mouth, from top to bottom, one corner to the other. This was the best dream he'd ever had! But then he suddenly woke up and realised what was happening to him. Jerry kept cool, offering Tom another delicious spoonful of the trifle. He wouldn't be able to resist, surely? *Mmmmm!* Jerry smacked his lips as he waved the creamy dollop just below Tom's nose.

For a moment Tom was sorely tempted, but then that cold alley flashed through his mind again. And the mangy dogs. Much to Jerry's surprise he suddenly swiped the spoon away and sprang from his basket. Terrified, Jerry ran for all he was worth back to his hole.

Although he just about made it, this was an even closer shave than before. He'd felt speedy Tom's breath on his neck, and the very tip of his tail had lost a few hairs. Tom had only been a whisker away from stamping on it! Still panting, Jerry went over to a mirror. There was only one thing for it. He would have to go on a diet himself...

Jerry managed not to eat a thing for one whole hour… then two… but at last his tummy began to rumble. *POY-OY-OY-ONG!* it gurgled. *PIY-IY-IY-ING!* He would have loved a piece of cheese now, but he had to be strict with himself. He couldn't let that Tom outrun him!

Jerry went to sleep without his usual cup of sugary cocoa, and when morning came he went without his breakfast as well. He was more hungry than he could ever remember, but at least he was sure that he was now more than a match for that awful Tom. The time had come to see if he was right…

Jerry ventured out of his hole, confidently making for Tom's basket. His foe was already awake, carefully measuring out some fat-free milk into his saucer. Jerry wondered how he could attract his attention, and he soon noticed the spoon in Tom's saucer. Its handle was overhanging the edge. A wide smile spread between his ears.

SPLAT! The milk went all over Tom's face as Jerry leap-frogged on to the end of the spoon.

Tom simply couldn't believe it. Wiping the mess away from his eyes, nose and whiskers, he stared down at Jerry's boldness. The mouse was *mad!* Was his memory that short? Had he forgotten that Tom had very nearly flattened him the last chase? And this one was likely to be even worse for him. Tom had now been on his diet for several more hours, and he was feeling *really* fit!

But Jerry stayed right where he was, refusing to scarper. He even seemed to have a certain smugness about him.

"Well, I'll soon wipe that grin off your face!" Tom thought as he pounced. Jerry just jumped clear of his claws, but he was by no means safe yet. There was a long, LONG way back to his mousehole! Tom grinned and started to run faster and faster - the wretched mouse didn't stand a chance!

Tom's legs were now turning like train wheels but for some reason he didn't seem to be getting any closer to Jerry. He just couldn't understand it. The little pest was running as fast as he was - maybe even faster! Tom made an almighty leap for him just before he reached his hole. But he completely missed and he slid along his tummy into the wall as Jerry smartly disappeared.

Tom gave his scorched tummy an irate rub. What had gone wrong? Why hadn't he caught him? He rubbed at his tummy again. TUMMY! Of course, that was it! The cheeky little pest must have gone on a diet as well!

Quick-thinking Tom immediately went to the fridge, looking for something to fatten Jerry up. There he saw Jerry's favourite cheese - perfect! No, that wouldn't do. Jerry would have seen it before and he hadn't been tempted *that* time. Then Tom gave a mischievous grin. Perhaps there *was* a way to make him eat it...

Tom couldn't believe how cunning he was as he stuck the huge wedge of cheese into a large mousetrap. He then placed the trap right outside Jerry's hole. Jerry wouldn't eat the cheese if Tom offered it, but he *might* if he saw it as a challenge!

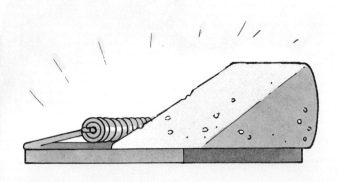

Tom tried not to snigger as he hid behind a chair, waiting for Jerry to pop out and investigate the cheese. The little pest would think he was so clever in working out that it was a trap. What he wouldn't realise was that it was a trap of a totally different sort!

Jerry soon appeared and started to sniff round the cheese. "What a pity I'm on a diet," he thought. He jumped back with horror on spotting the large spike through it and the strong trap spring ready to go off. With a shrug of the shoulders, he quickly returned towards his hole. Cheating that trap would be impossible. Or would it? He suddenly stopped with a thoughtful scratch of the head...

SNAP!

From behind his chair, Tom tittered. Everything was going nicely to plan!

Jerry picked up a discarded pencil and hurled it at the centre of the trap. It set off the spring and the heavy bar snapped down with such force that it shot the wedge of cheese up into the air. Jerry grinned as he caught it in both arms.

Tom grinned as well!

But then his devious plan went wrong. Jerry didn't stuff the cheese into his mouth as Tom had intended - but merely dropped it to the floor, unsampled. He gave a cheeky wink towards Tom's chair, patting his slim tummy as he sauntered back towards his hole!

Tom was *furious!* **THIS WAS WAR!**

Tom rushed back to his saucer and took what was left of the fat-free milk to the sink. He poured it down the plug-hole and filled the saucer with tap water instead. Then he tossed his slice of bread into the bin and took two flakes of wheat from the cupboard.

Jerry watched all this with alarm. That cat was soon going to be so slim that he could run a four minute mile! Well, if Tom could keep to a near-impossible diet, so could he! Jerry took the last remaining biscuit from his cupboard and crushed it into tiny crumbs. From now he would only eat one crumb a day. One a *week* if need be!

GURGLE

GURGLE

As the day drew to a close, Jerry's tummy was gurgling like a concrete mixer, and Tom's like a washing machine. They had never been so hungry before. But each was determined to be slimmer and faster than the other.

GURGLE

GURGLE

Soon after the housekeeper had gone to bed, they decided it was time to put their diets to the test. Jerry swaggered out of his hole, poking his tongue out at Tom. He walked right to the other end of the living room, wanting to give Tom a chance. But Tom wanted to give Jerry a chance as well. So, after darting in Jerry's direction, he skidded to a halt to allow him a good start.

Now the chase was on!

Jerry tore back towards his hole, with Tom a short distance behind. First, Tom closed the gap between them, then Jerry opened it again. Tom closed it once more, Jerry opened it. It was neck and neck.

But then Jerry suddenly started to flag.

"Got you!" Tom shrieked with glee as Jerry collapsed to the floor with exhaustion. But just as Tom was about to pounce, he felt his own energy drain away and collapsed to the floor himself!

"This is crazy!" Jerry panted as he weakly raised himself on to all fours. "We're so hungry, we can hardly move. Let's both go and raid the fridge and fatten ourselves up!"

Tom joyfully agreed. After all, he could hardly be any slower than he was now! So they both dragged their feeble bodies to the kitchen and opened the fridge door. Their tongues dropped right down to the floor at the sight of all that delicious food!

"This is much more fun than any old diet!" a bloated Jerry said an hour later as he munched on a huge slice of lemon meringue pie.

An equally bloated Tom nodded his head and licked a great dollop of cream from his lips. There was only one thing that spoiled his happiness - the end of the week was only another day away and he would be out on the street!

"Don't worry about that!" Jerry reassured him. "I've eaten so much tonight that I won't need to come out of my hole again for a month. The housekeeper will think you have eaten me." He chuckled as he glanced at Tom's huge tummy. "You can tell her that's what that great big bulge is!"

Carnival
An imprint of the Children's Division
of the Collins Publishing Group
8 Grafton Street, London W1X 3LA

Published by Carnival 1990

© 1990 Turner Ent. Co. All rights reserved.
Licensed by Copyright Promotions Ltd

ISBN 0 00 193209 8

Printed in Great Britain by
BPCC Paulton Books Limited